# WHY ARE THEY KNEELING?

## Damon Wyatt Thornton
### Illustrated by: Bryan Brown

D1400512

# DEDICATION

To Damon, Mil, Kaylin, Nathaniel, Joshua, Destynee, Jeremiah, Kendrick, Aydan, Kristine, Mallory, and all of the Courageous Kids around the world who are brave enough to be different, ask questions, and force us to be better, and to every adult who continues to nurture, love, and encourage the courageousness of our kids, this book is dedicated to you.

# ACKNOWLEDGMENTS

I would like to first give thanks to GOD, because without HIM, nothing is possible.  I would also like to thank HIM for my support system.  Thank you Kiamesha, Marsha, Taisha, Brian, Trayvonia, Chelsie and everyone else who has been placed on assignment to love and support me.  Each of you has helped me become courageous enough to step out on faith and chase my dreams.

# WHY ARE THEY KNEELING?

## Damon Wyatt Thornton
### Illustrated by: Bryan Brown

Hooray! Hooray! It's Sunday funday!
Today is for football, family, friends, and food.

My whole family is here, and we are all
in a sports mood!

2

I thought, "I love this day, watching
my favorite  players lined up on the field.
Stretching, tossing, running.
Arms made out of steel."
I grabbed a seat next to my mom so
that I could watch the drills.

3

But then something happened that made
me stand very, very still!

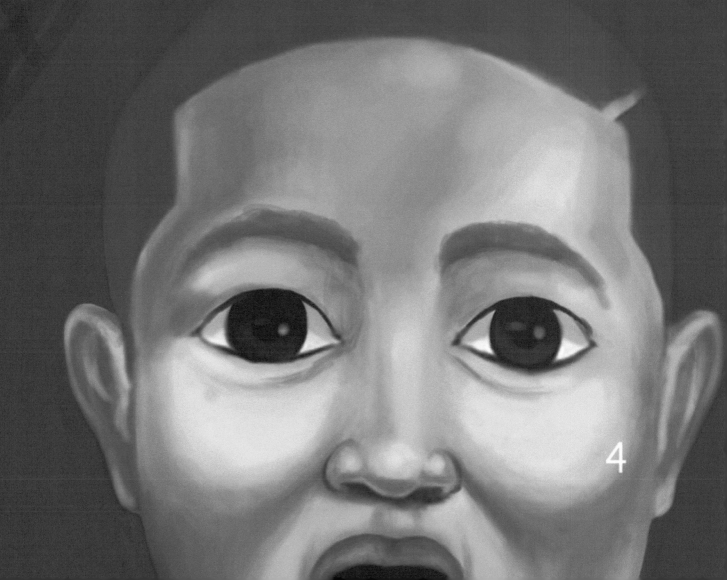

4

All of my favorite players together I spotted on TV. Bend their legs and kneel way down, Mom, "Why did they take a knee?"

"Why are they kneeling during
our country's song?"
My dad replied, "It's a way to speak out
against something that is wrong!"

I thought for a while, and I knew exactly what I would do. Could I take a knee just like them if I saw something wrong, too?

7

My grandma said,
"Absolutely, but it's not the only way!
I used to do sit-ins and marches way
back in my day!"

8

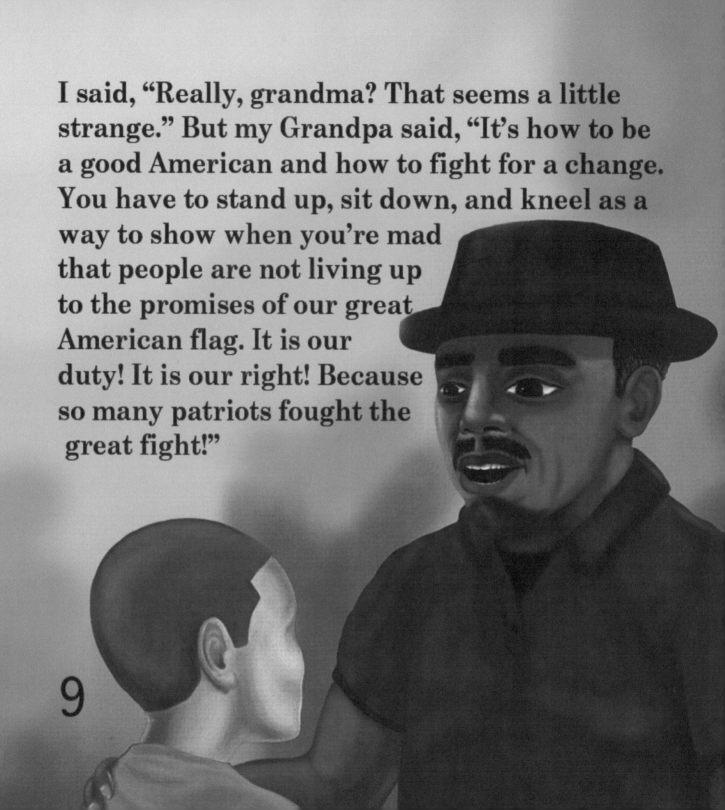

I said, "Really, grandma? That seems a little strange." But my Grandpa said, "It's how to be a good American and how to fight for a change. You have to stand up, sit down, and kneel as a way to show when you're mad that people are not living up to the promises of our great American flag. It is our duty! It is our right! Because so many patriots fought the great fight!"

9

I asked, "If it's the right thing, then why are some
so upset?" My mother said, "Well, everyone
won't be excited when you learn to protest.
They might be scared, just not know,
or have different beliefs because
their parents told them so."

10

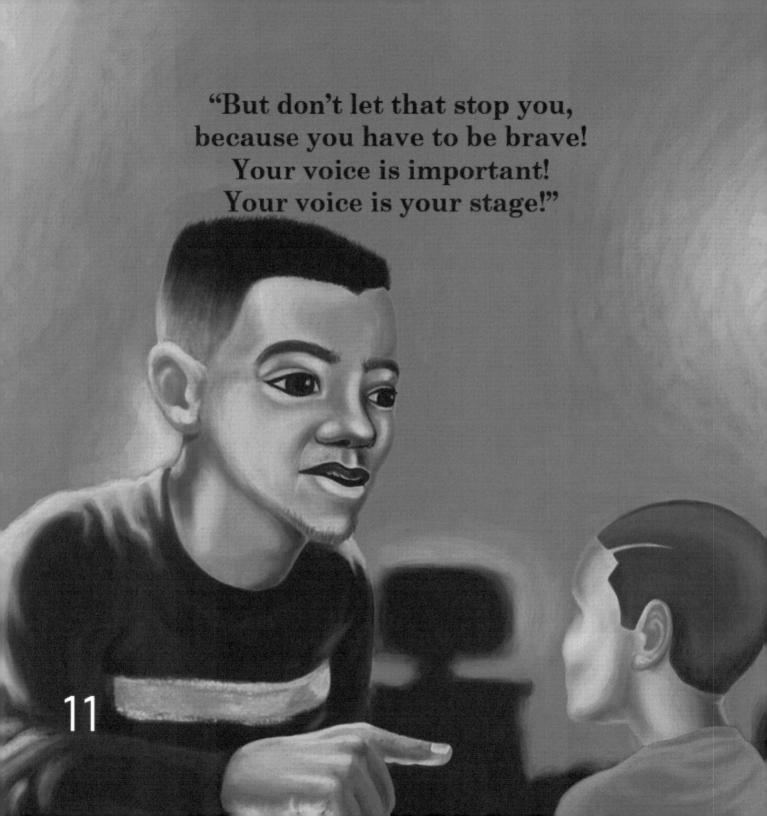

"I would like to take a knee,
but I don't want to stop there.
I want to change the world,
because you have raised me to care."

12

"How you do it is up to you, fight for what is right. Don't worry about people's opinion or if people will agree. Just find your way in this world to take your own knee."

13

I can write a letter to
my teacher!

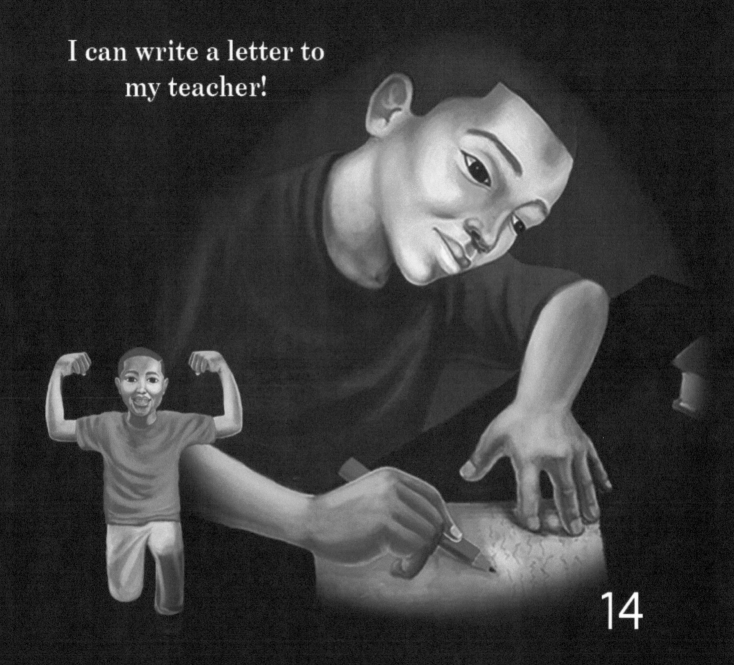

14

Or hold a sign in the bleachers!

15

I also love to sing, so maybe
I'll write a song!

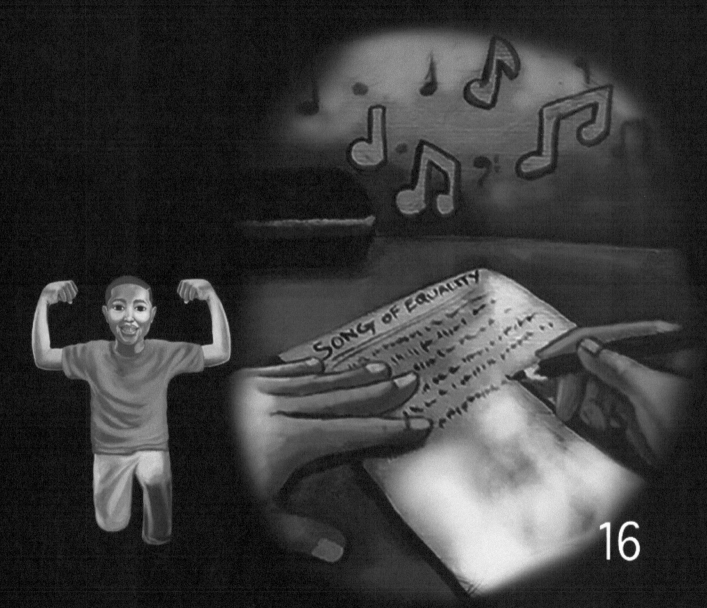

Or not buy candy from the store
that tries to treat us wrong!

17

I can give my allowance to a cause
that I think is great!

Or form a group with friends and
march-as long as I'm back for grace!

19

So as the game started, I looked from team
to team. I realized in that moment, I had a
new dream. I want to fight for what is right,
so that we all have a choice. Speaking up for all
that is good is how I will use my voice!

20

As I looked around at my family,
my heart was filled with glee,

21

that my favorite player cared enough about my country to stop and take a knee.

22

# Courageous kids ask questions!
## What questions do you have?

# Courageous kids change the world!
## Write down some of the courageous ways you will change the world.

# THE END!

## LET'S CONTINUE THIS CONVERSATION!

We are really excited to be sharing this book with you but we are more excited about the conversation that will come from it. Please follow us on Instagram **@courageouskidstories**. We want to hear from you so leave your comments, feedback, and pictures and videos of you reading and discussing this book. Use the hashtag **#courageouskidstories** so we can share your pictures and videos with our Courageous Kid community!

CPSIA information can be obtained
at www.ICGtesting.com
Printed in the USA
LVHW071726020419
612711LV00011B/226/P

*  9  7  8  0  9  9  7  9  6  2  1  0  9  *